Space

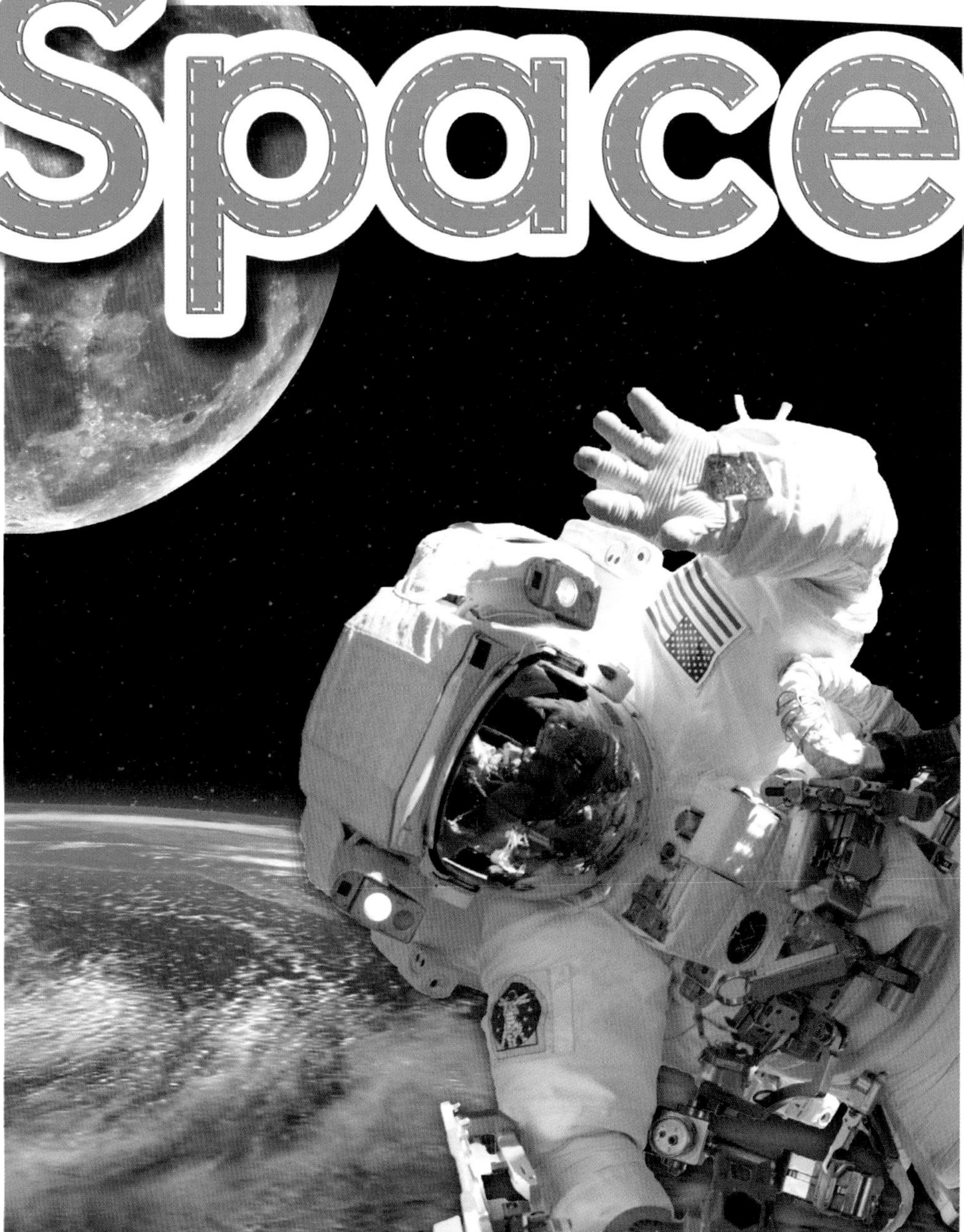

Stephanie Reid

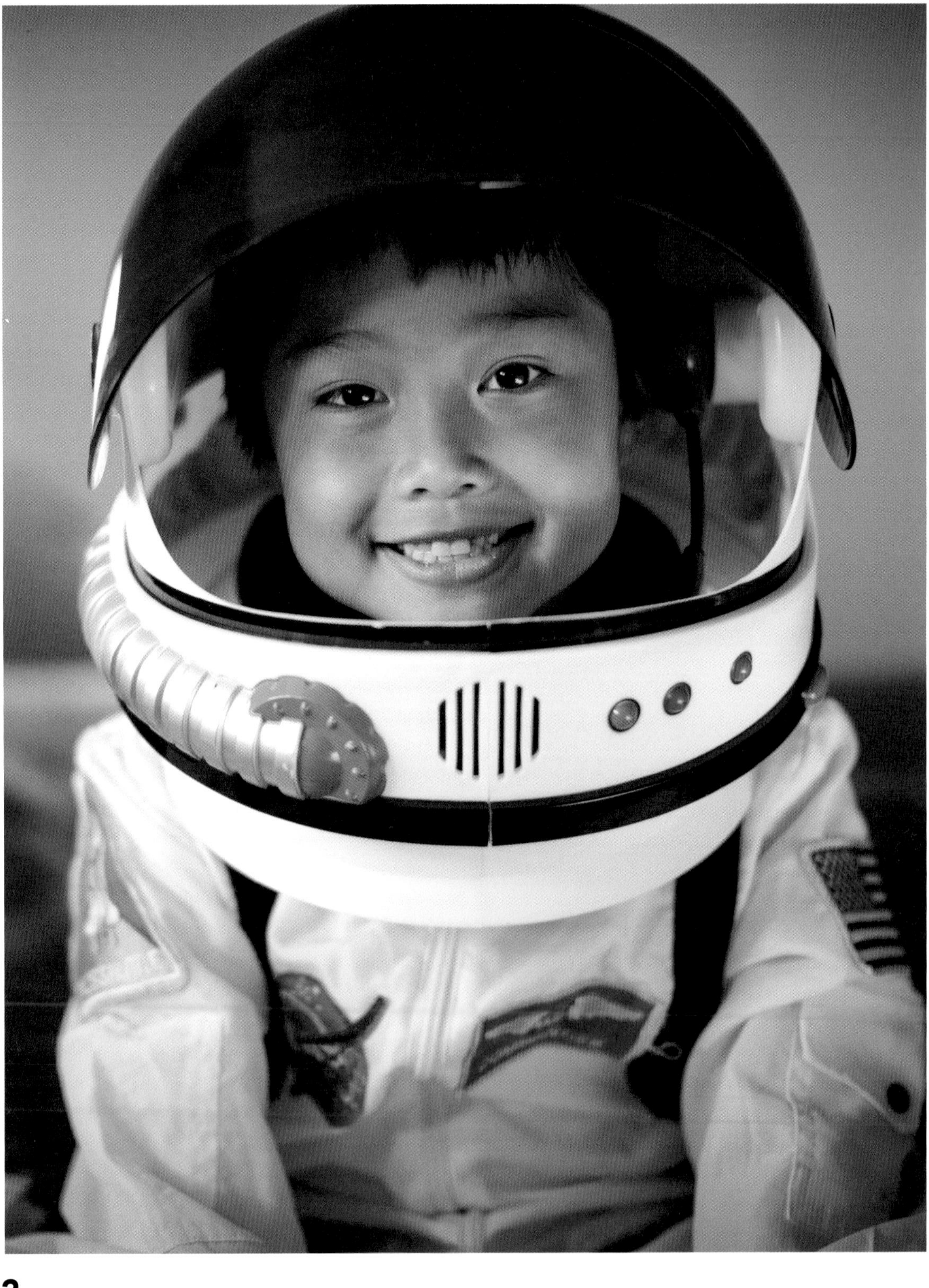

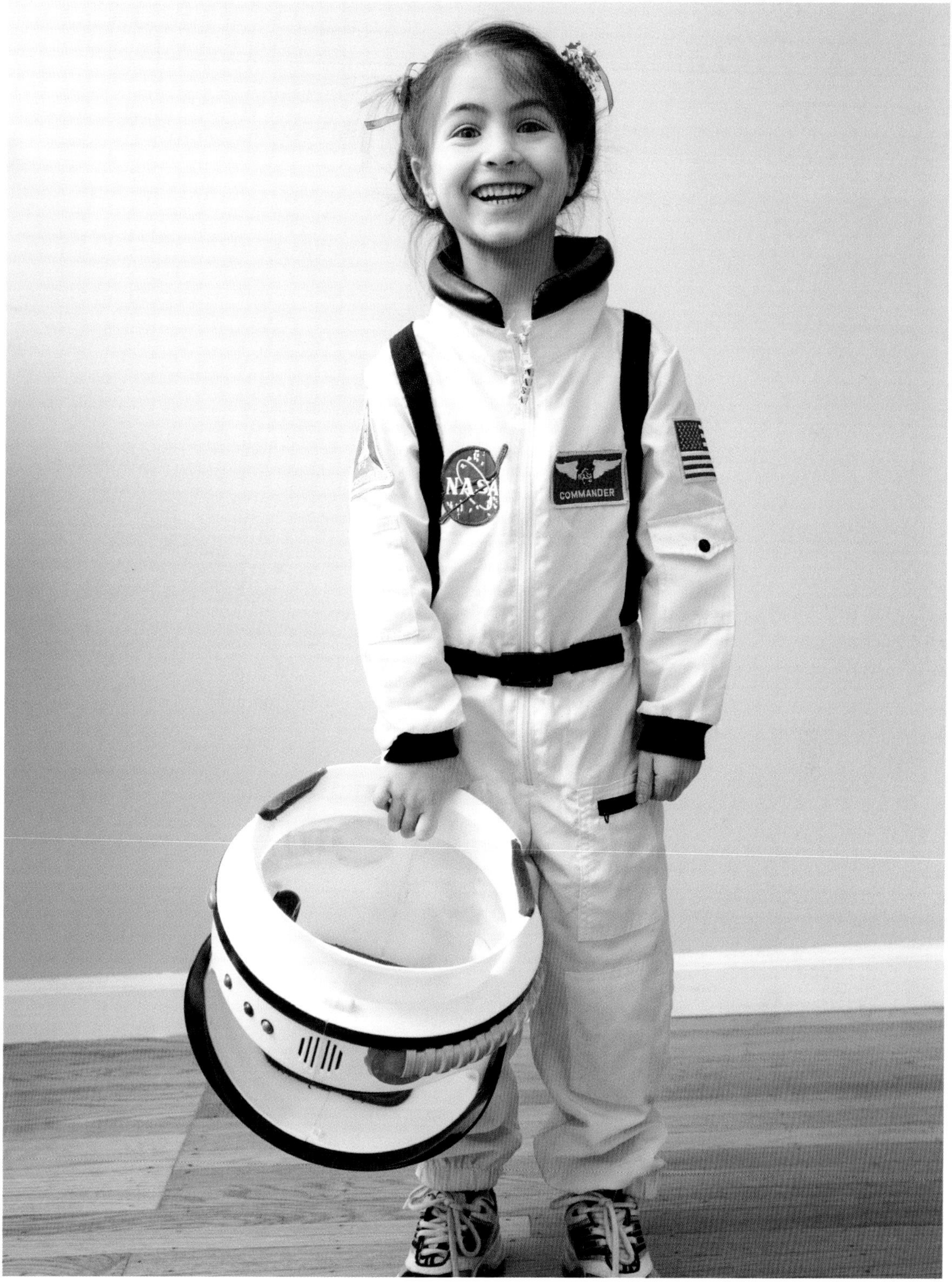
NASA
COMMANDER

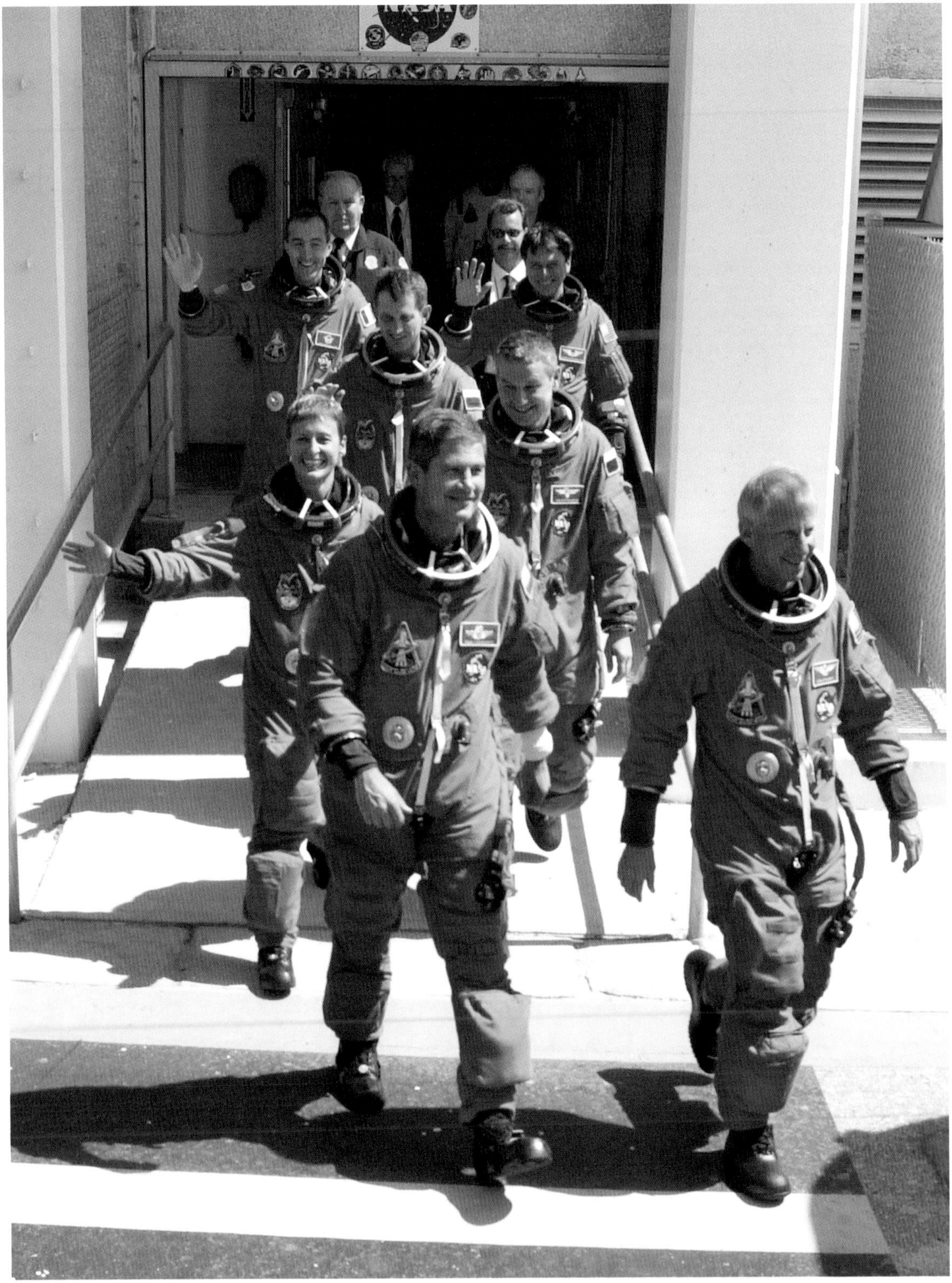

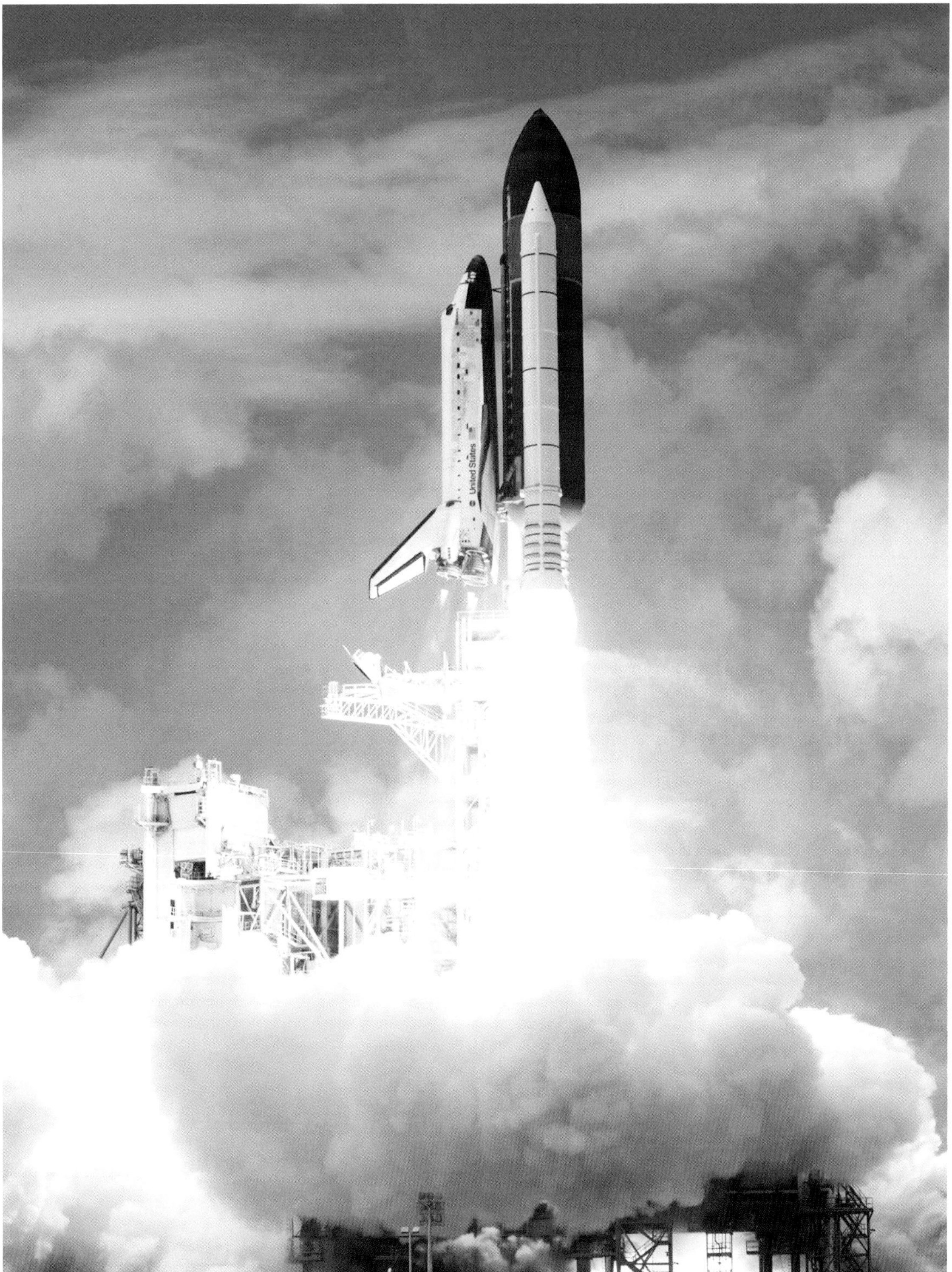
United States

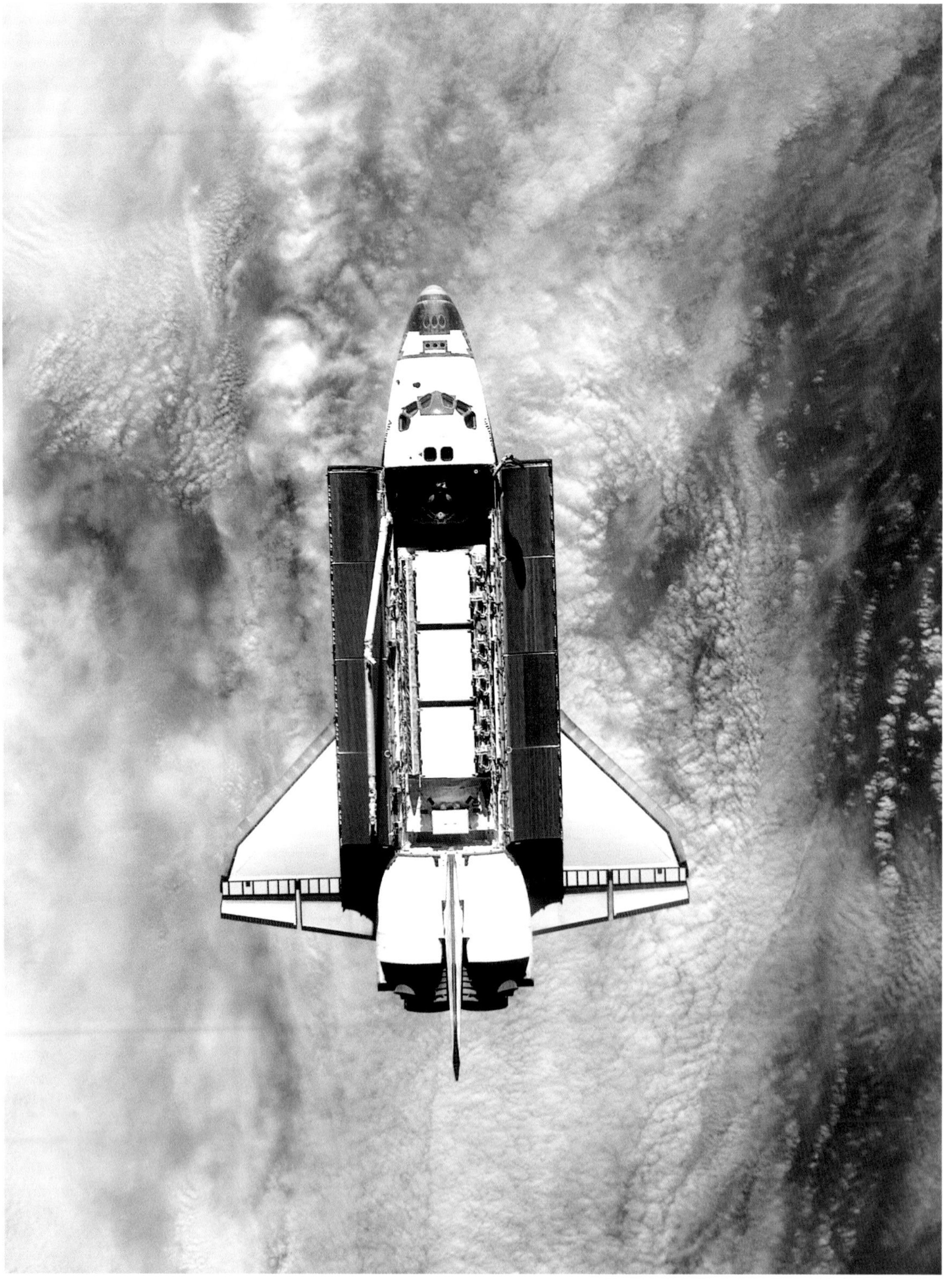

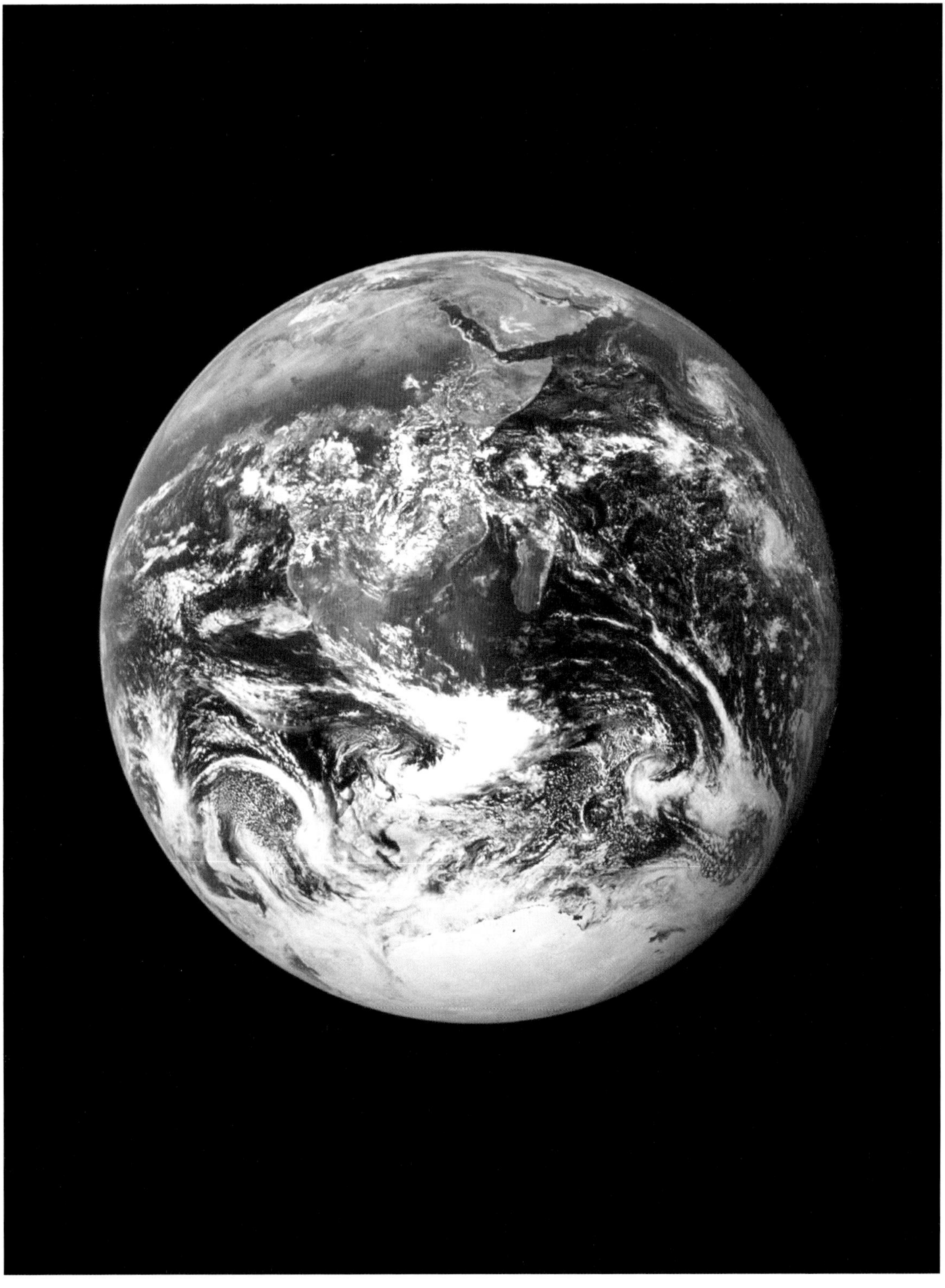

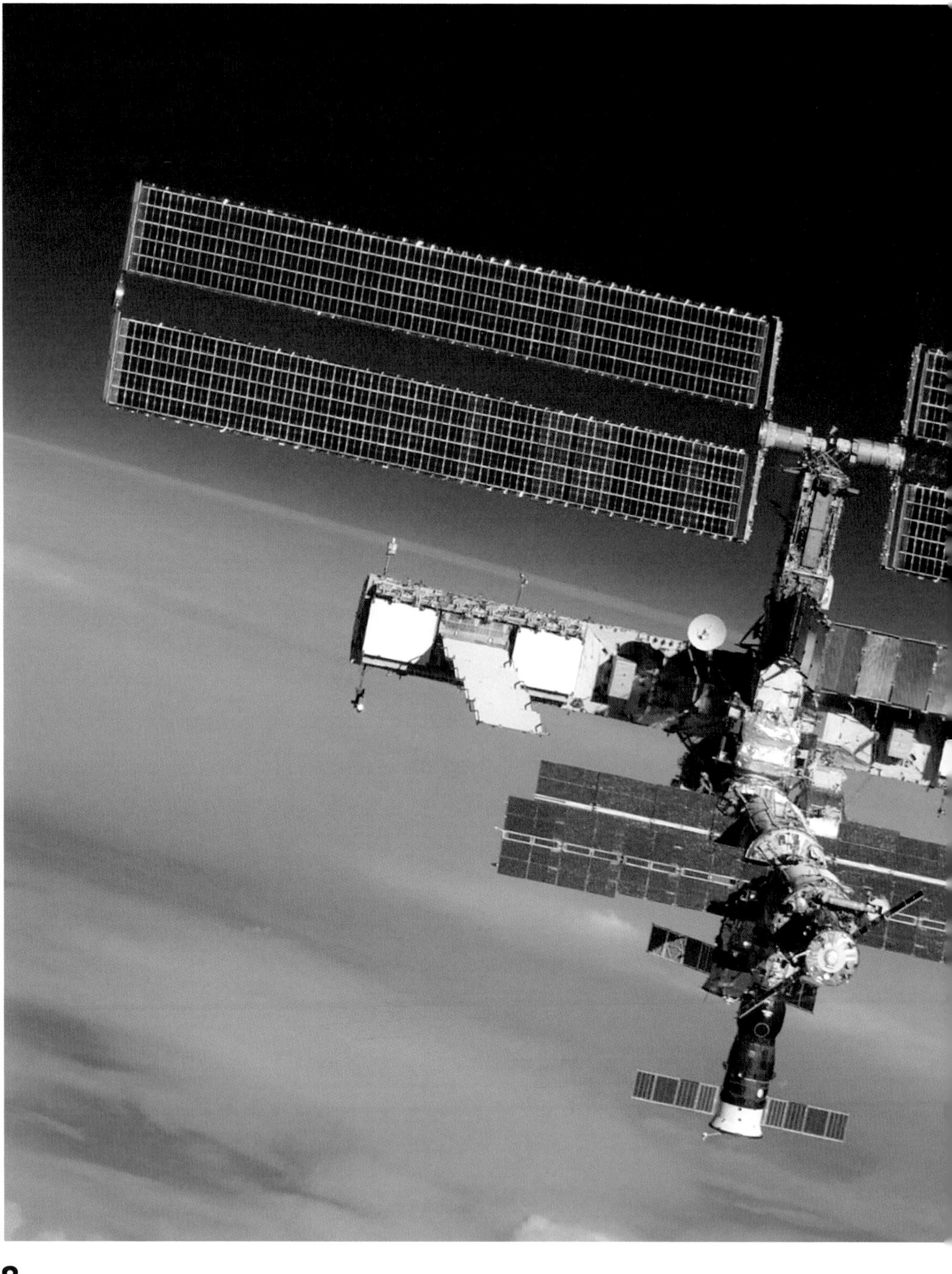

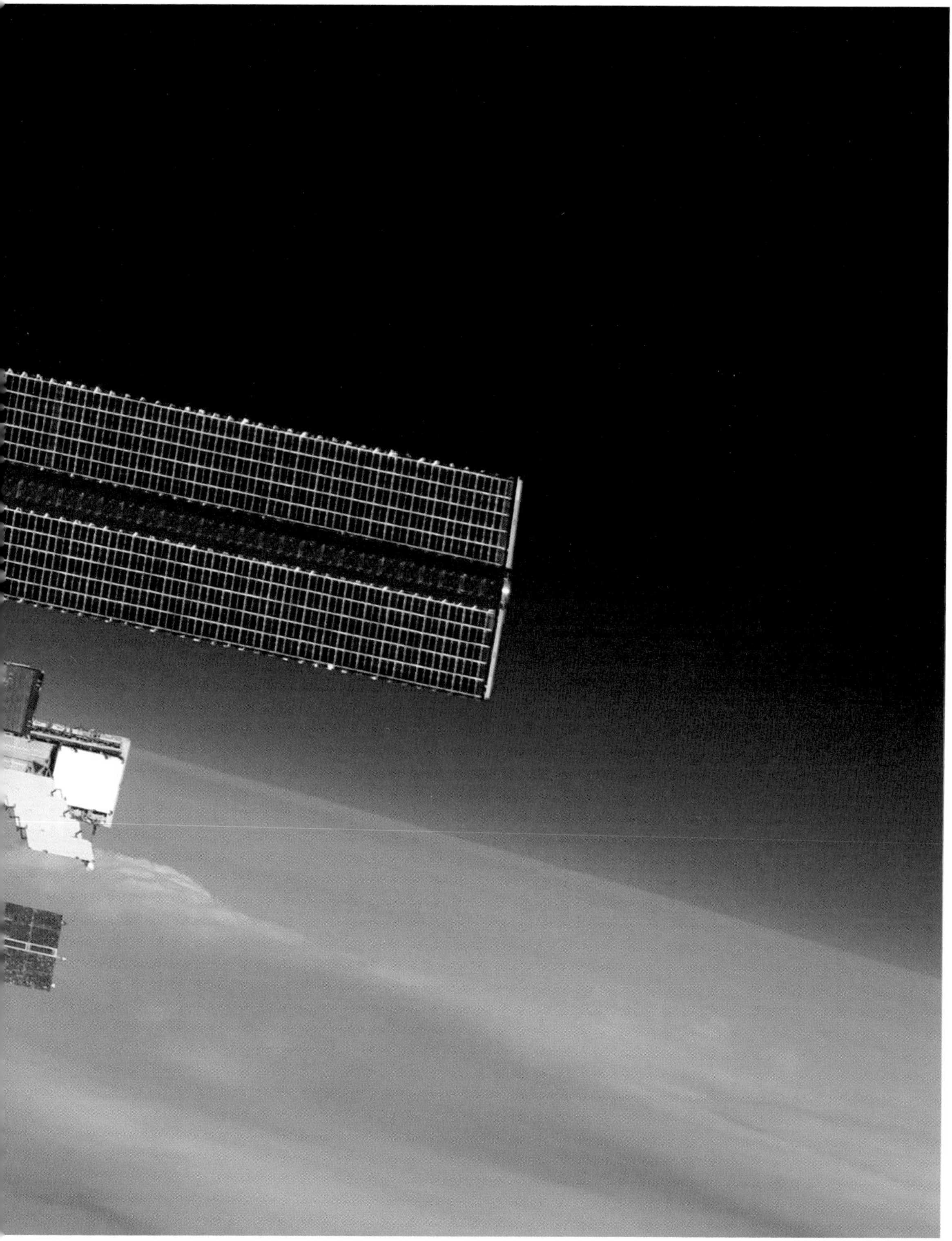

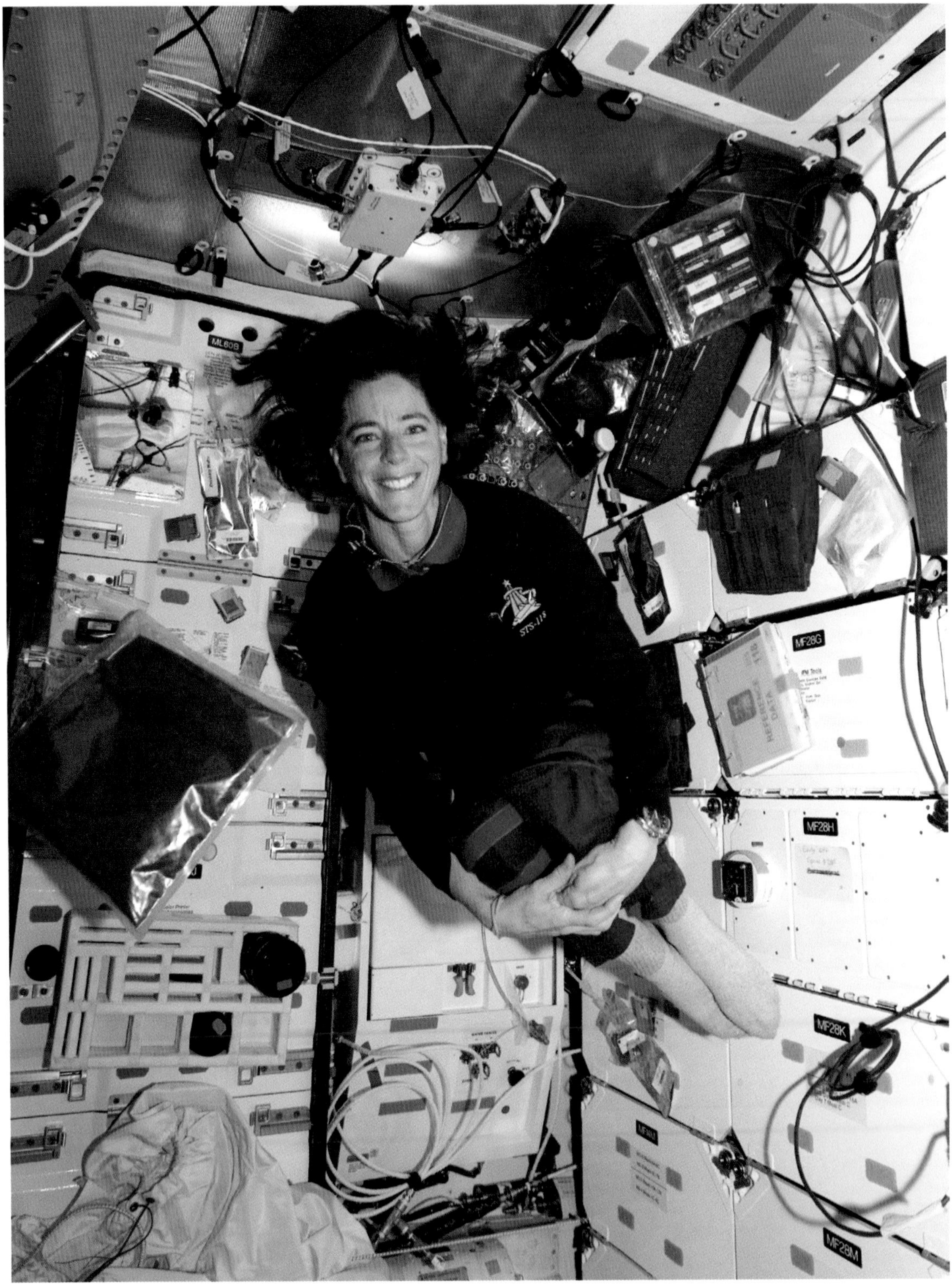
ML60B
STS-118
MF28G
REFERENCE DATA
MF28H
MF28K
MF28M

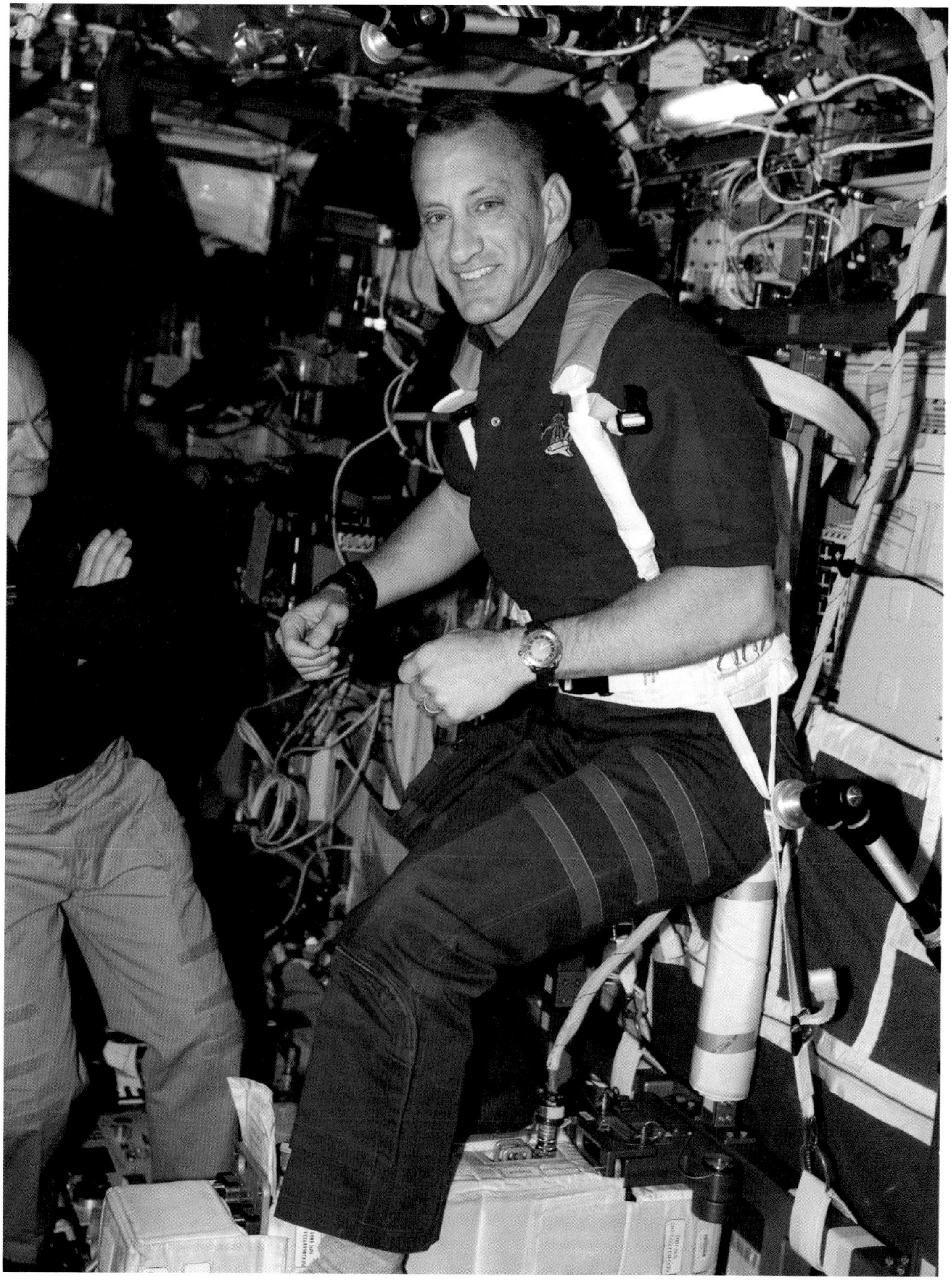

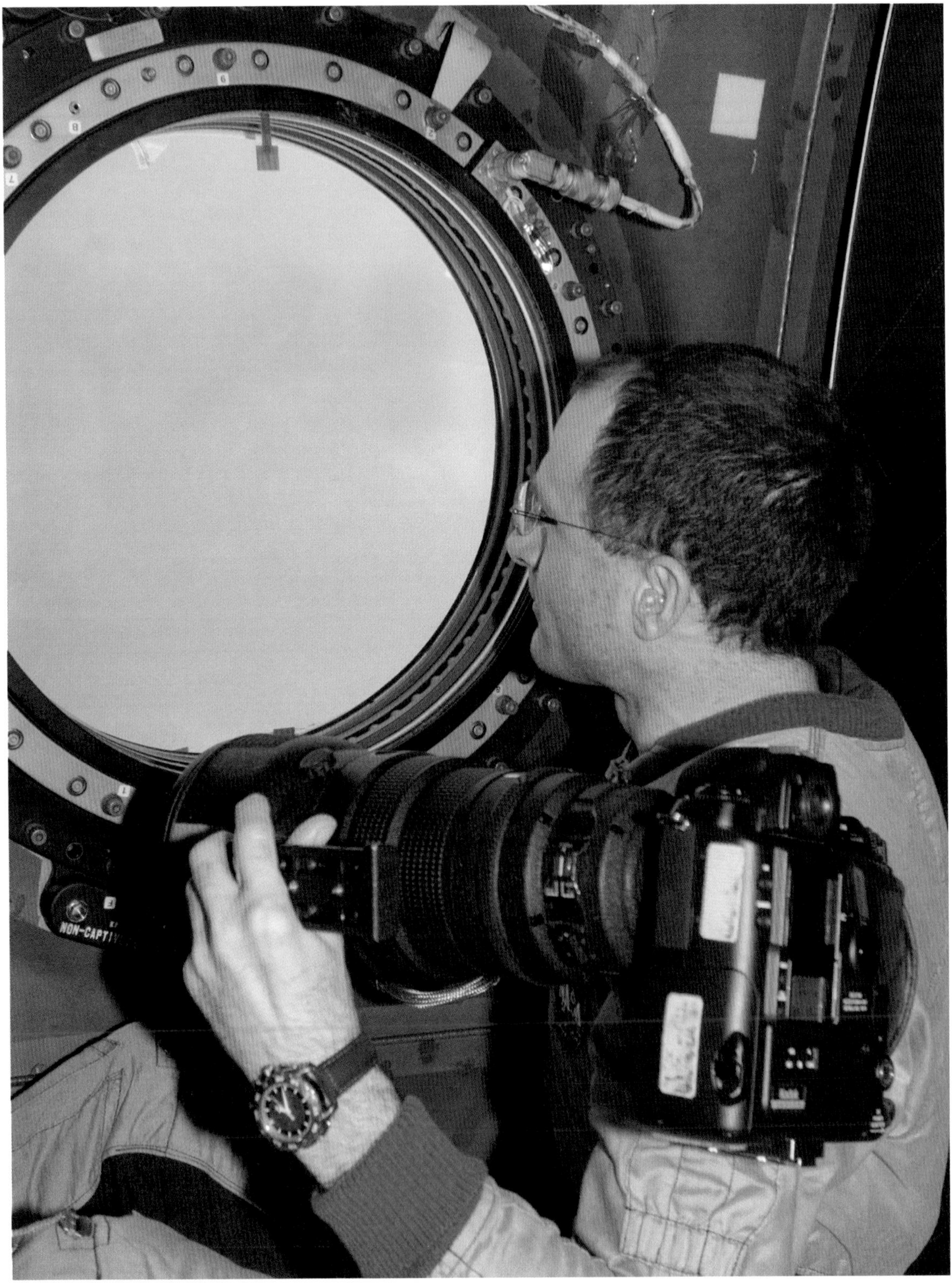

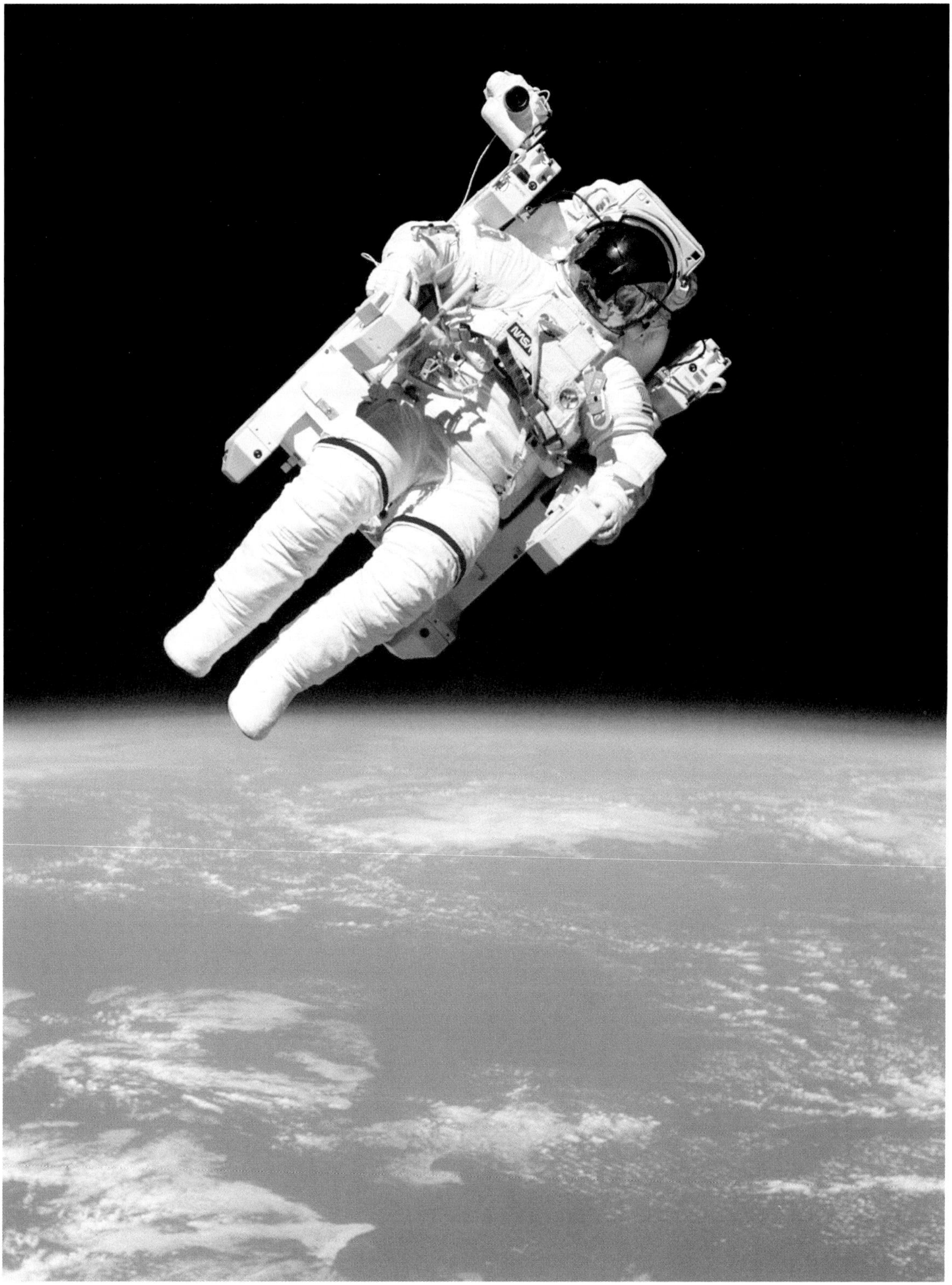

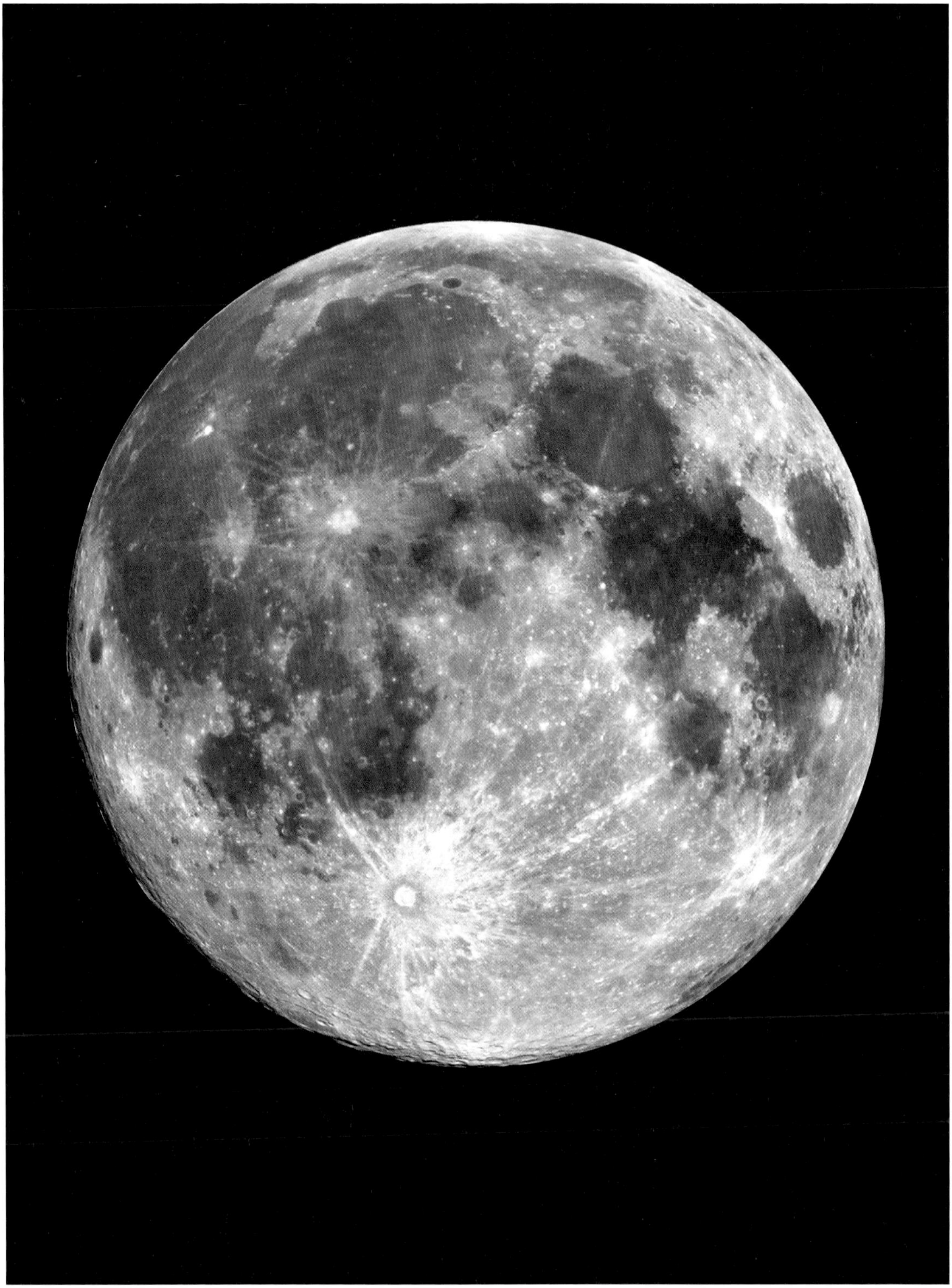

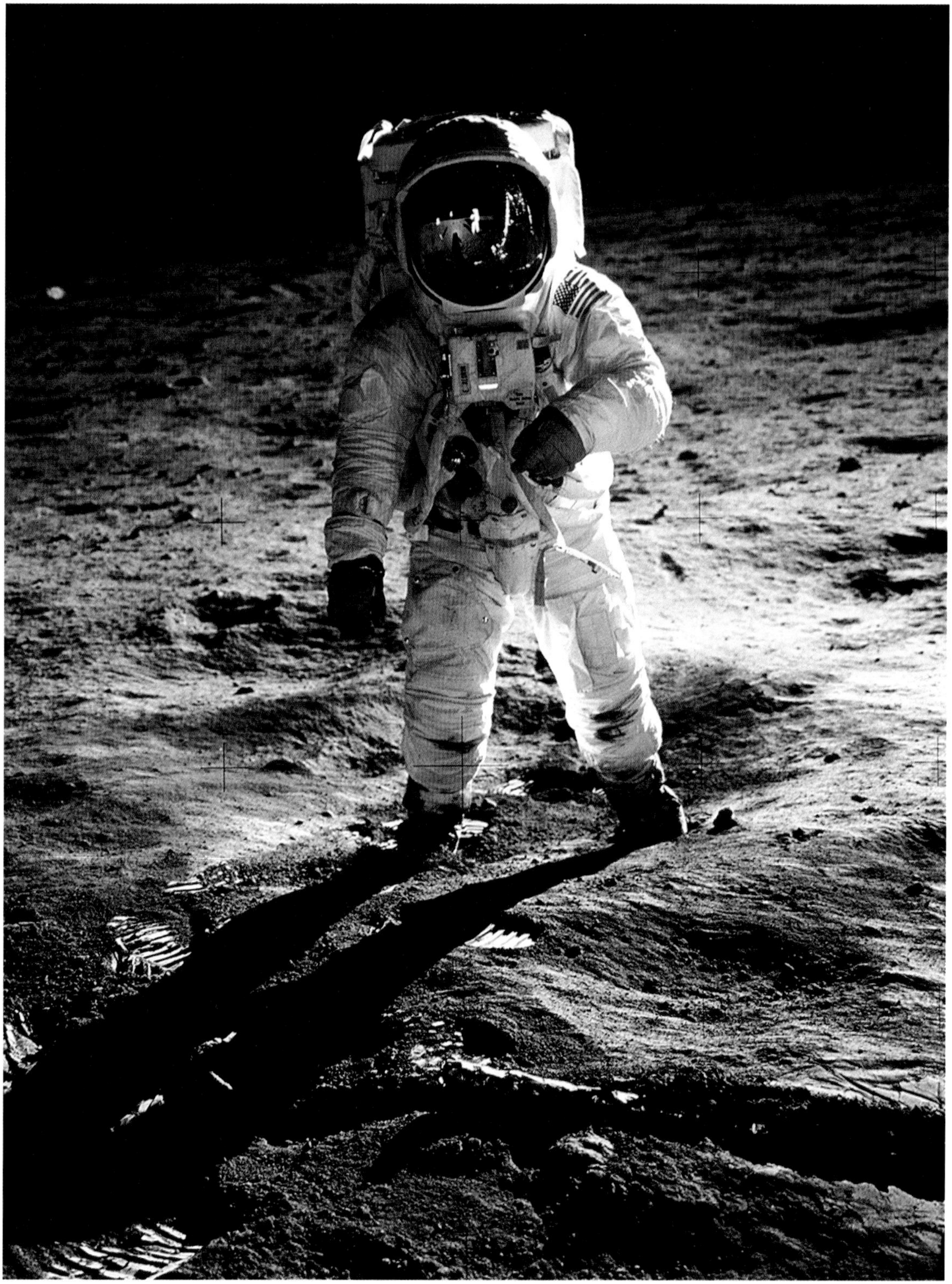

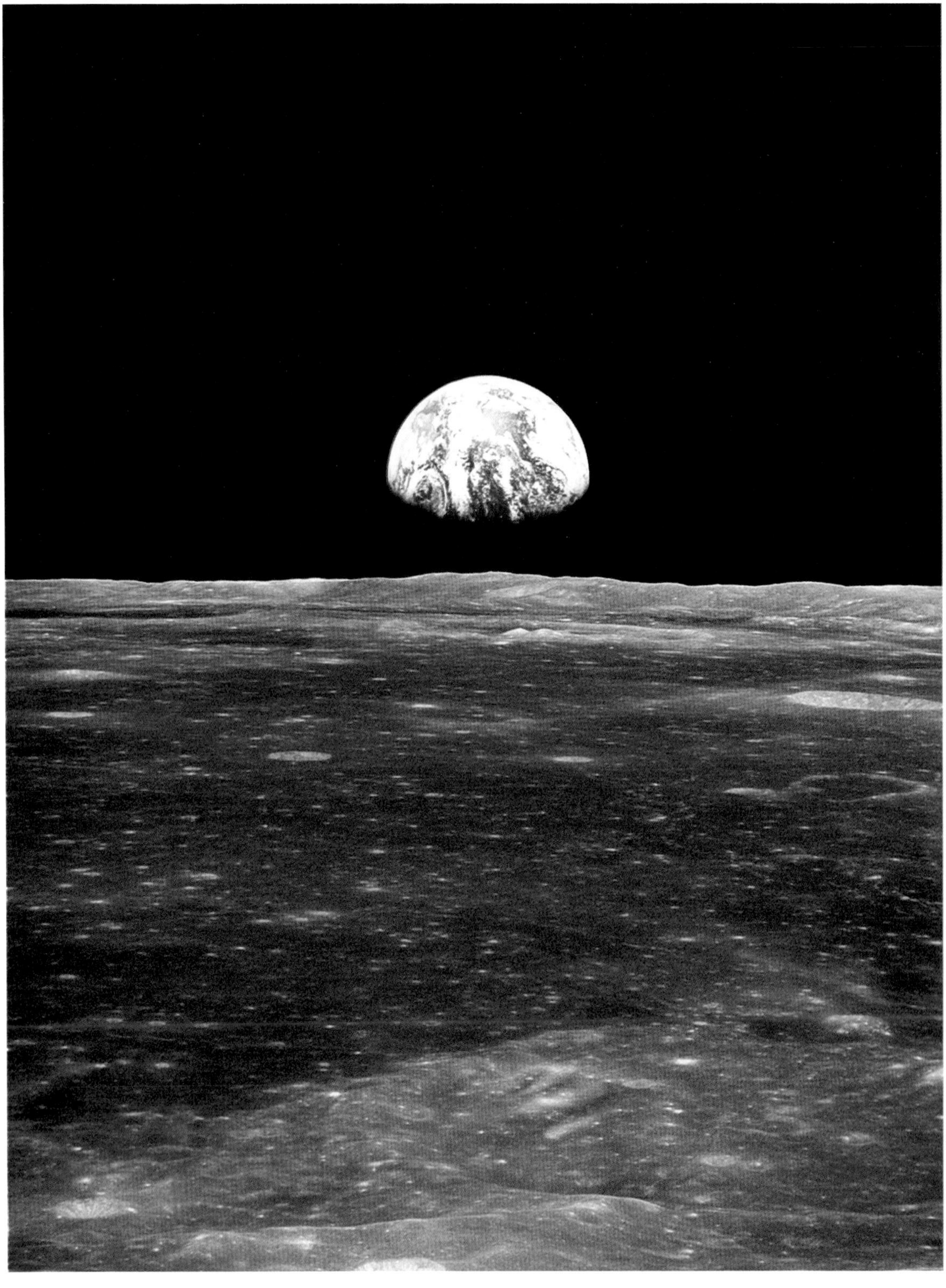